Hokey Pokey:

Another Prickly
Love Story

by LISA WHEELER

Illustrated by JANIE BYNUM

 LITTLE, BROWN AND COMPANY

New York · Boston

Also by Lisa Wheeler:
Bubble Gum, Bubble Gum
Porcupining
Te Amo, Bebé, Little One

Also illustrated by Janie Bynum:
Porcupining
Rock-a-Baby Band
Bathtub Blues

For my daughter, Kelly, who loves to dance.
— Love, L.W.

To little dancers everywhere — keep dancing,
no matter what. And to Lisa Wheeler, a
great dance partner in books.
—J.B.

Text copyright © 2006 by Lisa Wheeler
Illustrations copyright © 2006 by Janie Bynum

Little, Brown and Company

Time Warner Book Group
1271 Avenue of the Americas, New York, NY 10020
Visit our Web site at www.lb-kids.com

First Edition: January 2006

Library of Congress Cataloging-in-Publication Data

Wheeler, Lisa, 1963-
  Hokey Pokey: another prickly love story / by Lisa Wheeler ; illustrated
by Janie Bynum.—1st ed.
      p. cm.
  Summary: After a series of discouraging dance teachers, Cushion the
porcupine finds his rhythm with his true love Barb.
  ISBN 0-316-00090-6
  [1. Dance—Fiction. 2. Porcupines—Fiction. 3. Hedgehogs—Fiction.] I.
Title: Porcupining sequel. II. Bynum, Janie, ill. III. Title.
PZ7.W5657Pr 2005
[E]—dc22   2004007840

            10 9 8 7 6 5 4 3 2 1

                    PHX

            Printed in China

The illustrations for this book were done in digital watercolor and pastel.
The text was set in Schneidler and Aunt Mildred.

Cushion was a porcupine with a problem.

He *really* loved Barb
and Barb *really* loved to dance.
And that was the problem.

Cushion's rumba was rumpled,

his waltz always wobbled,

and his tango was totally tangled.

"One step...two step...three step...four.
Pick my tail up off the floor."

But since Barb loved to dance,
and Cushion loved Barb,
he went poking around the petting zoo,
hoping to learn some dance steps.

First, he hot-footed it over to the foxes' den.

"Tally-ho!" Cushion called to his fox friend. "I want to learn to dance. Will you teach me to fox-trot?"

"You are certainly not a fox," said Tally-ho, "and I have never seen a porcupine trot. But I shall try to teach you."

Cushion sang a dancing song to help him keep in step.

"One step...two step...three step...four.
Trot my feet across the floor.
See me trotting? Watch me go!
I can do it! Trot-trot..."

"NO!"

But it was too late.
Cushion had trotted right over Tally-ho's bushy tail.
"OWOOOOO!" howled Tally-ho.
"Oops!" said Cushion. "Sorry."
"My poor tail!" said the fox. "You are a menace to decent society!"

"No point in sticking around here," said Cushion,
backing out of the den.
"Maybe I'll have better luck with the rabbits."

Cushion found Clover outside her hutch.

"I need to learn to dance," said Cushion. "Will you teach me the bunny hop?"

"Well, you're not a bunny," said Clover, "and porcupines don't hop. But I can *try* to teach you."

Cushion sang his dancing song as he followed Clover's lead.

"One step...two step...three step...four.
Hop myself across the floor.
Bounce, bounce, bounce until you drop.
I can do it! Hop-hop..."

"STOP!"

But it was too late.

Cushion had hopped right onto Clover's foot.

"OUCHIES!" Clover cried.

"Uh-oh," said Cushion. "Sorry."

"I knew it!" said Clover. "You are a dancing disaster!"

"I guess rabbits' feet aren't always so lucky," said Cushion as he walked away.

"Maybe I'd better try my feathered friends."

Biddy was alone in the henhouse.

"I *have* to learn to dance," said Cushion.

"Will you teach me the funky chicken?"

"You're not a chicken," said Biddy, "and you sure don't know funky."

"PLEASE!" cried Cushion. "I can't trot, and I can't hop, and I want to dance with Barb."

"Don't get so ruffled," said Biddy. "I'll teach you some of my moves."

Cushion sang his dancing song as
Biddy showed him the steps.

"One step...two step...three step...four.
Flap my wings across the floor.
Shake it fast and shake it slow.

I can do it! Flap-flap..."

"WHOA!"

But it was too late.

Cushion had flapped right into Biddy's backside.

"BAWK UP! BAWK UP!" Biddy clucked.

"My fault," said Cushion. "Sorry."

"My bottom looks like a dartboard!" said Biddy. "You're a cluck-cluck-clutz!"

"Time for me to fly the coop,"
said Cushion as he hurried out
of the henhouse.

Cushion headed back toward home.
His tail dragged in the dirt.
His quills drooped on his back.
He felt lower than a limbo stick.

"I really wanted to dance," said Cushion. "But it's pointless. There is no one left to teach me."

"I can teach you," said a sweet, clear voice behind him.

"Barb!" cried Cushion. "Do you really mean it? Can you teach me to dance?"

"I surely can-can!" said Barb. "Then we can dance together."

So Barb taught Cushion the fox trot...

and the bunny hop...

and even the funky chicken.

"I saved the best for last," said Barb. "Now we can try my favorite dance of all."

That night, Cushion learned the Hokey Pokey and he turned himself around, dancing the night away with his best friend.

'Cause that's what it's all about!

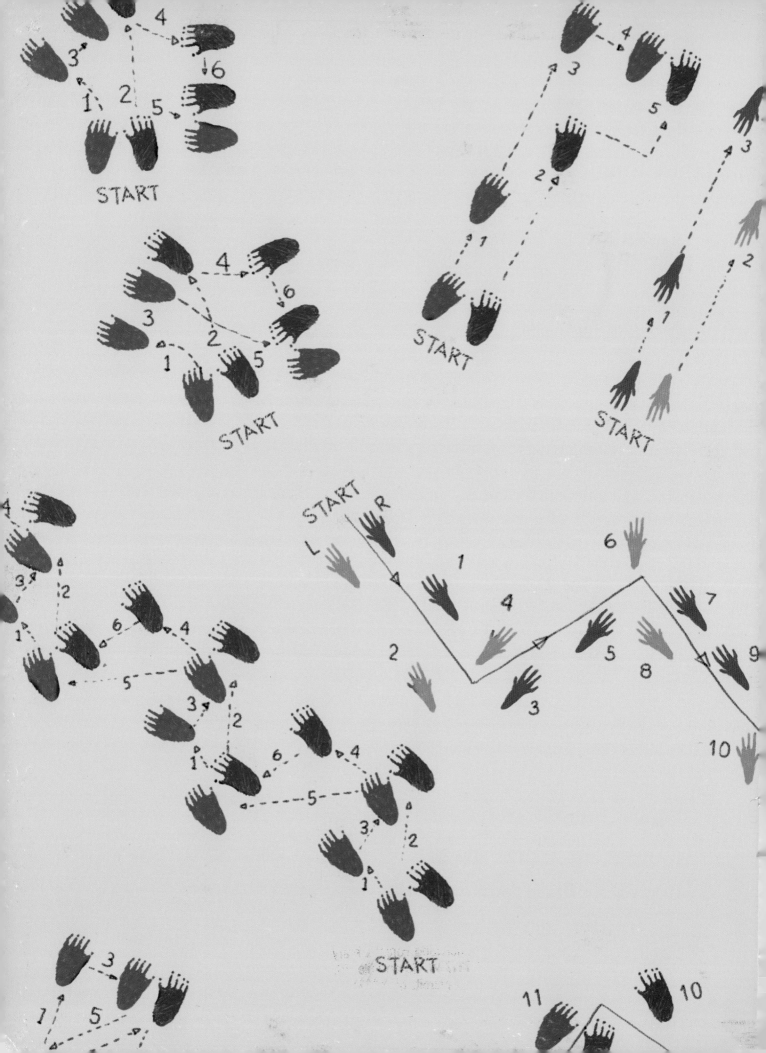